She'll be comin' round the mountain /
E Sch   149202

She'll Be
Comin' Round the Mountain

Book copyright © 2007 Trudy Corporation and the Smithsonian Institution, Washington, DC 20560.

Published by Soundprints, an imprint of Trudy Corporation, Norwalk, Connecticut.

Book design: Konrad Krukowski
Editor: Barbie Heit Schwaeber
Production Editor: Brian E. Giblin

First edition 2007
10 9 8 7 6 5 4 3 2 1
Printed in China

Acknowledgments:
   Soundprints would like to thank Ellen Nanney and Katie Mann at the Smithsonian Institution's Office of Product Development and Licensing for their help in the creation of this book.

   A portion of the proceeds from your purchase of this licensed product supports the stated educational mission of the Smithsonian Institution - "the increase and diffusion of knowledge."

Library of Congress Cataloging-in-Publication Data is on file with the publisher and the Library of Congress.

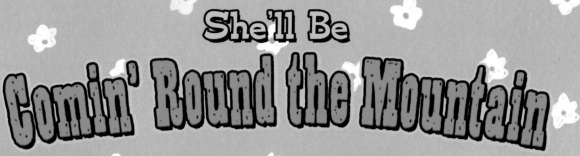

She'll Be Comin' Round the Mountain

Edited by Barbie H. Schwaeber
Illustrated by Suzanne Beaky

Soundprints
Where Children Discover...

She'll be comin' round the mountain
when she comes—**Here she comes!**
She'll be comin' round the mountain
when she comes—**Here she comes!**

She'll be comin' round the mountain
  she'll be comin' round the mountain
She'll be comin' round the mountain
  when she comes—**Here she comes!**

She'll be driving six white horses
 when she comes—**Whoa, back!**
She'll be driving six white horses
 when she comes—**Whoa, back!**
She'll be driving six white horses
 she'll be driving six white horses
She'll be driving six white horses
 when she comes—**Whoa, back!**

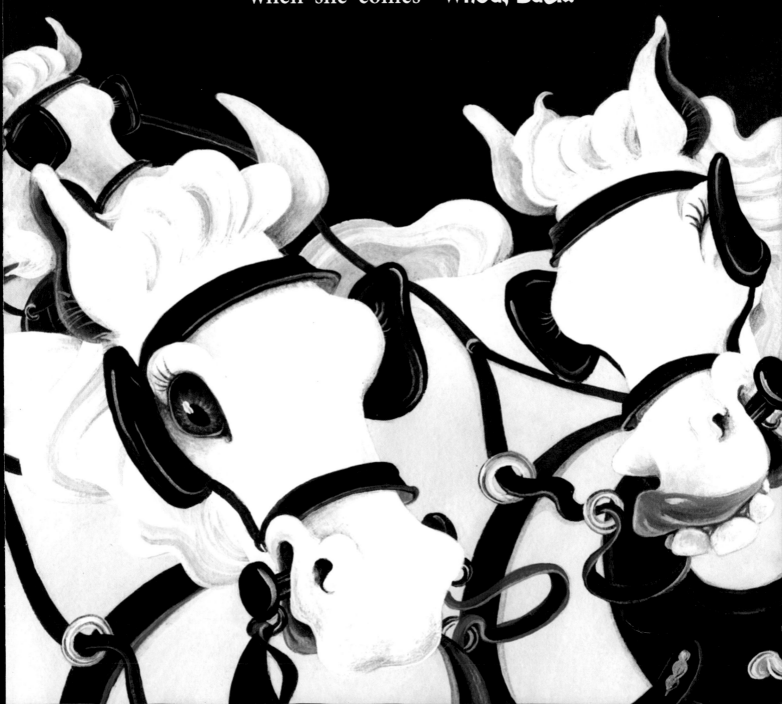

Oh, we'll all go out to meet her
when she comes—**Hi, Babe!**
Oh, we'll all go out to meet her
when she comes—**Hi, Babe!**
Oh, we'll all go out to meet her
we'll all go out to meet her
We'll all go out to meet her
when she comes—**Hi, Babe!**

She'll be wearing red pajamas
    when she comes—**Scratch, scratch!**
She'll be wearing red pajamas
    when she comes—**Scratch, scratch!**
She'll be wearing red pajamas
    she'll be wearing red pajamas
She'll be wearing red pajamas
    when she comes—**Scratch, scratch!**

She will have to sleep with Grandma
when she comes—**Oh, no!**
She will have to sleep with Grandma
when she comes—**Oh, no!**
She will have to sleep with Grandma
she will have to sleep with Grandma
She will have to sleep with Grandma
when she comes—**Oh, no!**

We will all have chicken and dumplings
when she comes—**Yum! Yum!**
We will all have chicken and dumplings
when she comes—**Yum! Yum!**
We will all have chicken and dumplings
we will all have chicken and dumplings
We will all have chicken and dumplings
when she comes—**Yum! Yum!**

Here she comes!
Whoa, back!
Hi, Babe!
Scratch, scratch!
Oh, No!
Yum, Yum!

She'll be comin' round the mountain
  when she comes
She'll be comin' round the mountain
  when she comes
She'll be comin' round the mountain
  she'll be comin' round the mountain

She'll be comin' round the mountain
when she comes!

NOTES AND NOSTALGIA

No one exactly knows where folk songs come from, but it seems that "She'll Be Comin' Round the Mountain" can be traced back to a spiritual song called "When the Chariot Comes." Like many folk songs, the words have changed over the years, but the original feeling of the song, a message of hope and determination, remains the same.

"She'll Be Comin' Round the Mountain" is believed to have been written during the late 1800's, but the song was printed in the 1927 version of Carl Sandburg's "The American Songbag." Carl Sandburg was an American poet and biographer who enjoyed collecting and performing folk songs.

In the 1890's, as America began to expand, "She'll Be Comin' Round the Mountain" became popular among railroad workers in the Midwestern United States. Some people think that the "she" in the opening line of the song is a train traveling for the first time on the workers' newly-laid train tracks.

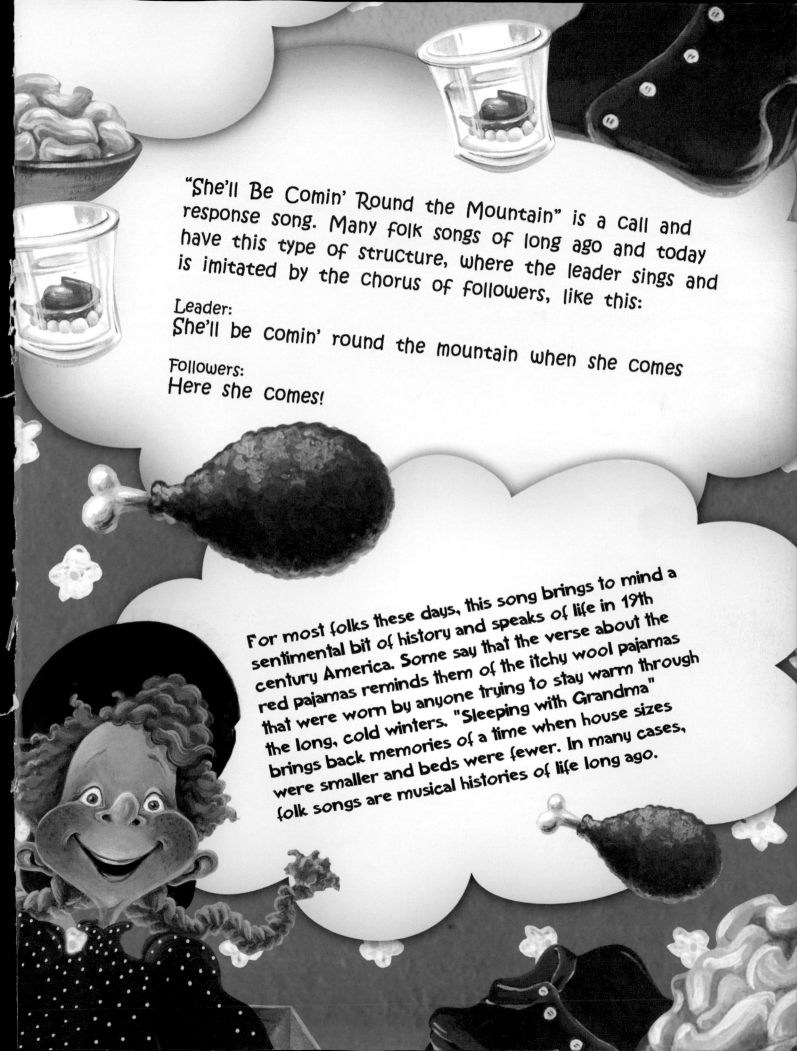

"She'll Be Comin' Round the Mountain" is a call and response song. Many folk songs of long ago and today have this type of structure, where the leader sings and is imitated by the chorus of followers, like this:

Leader:
She'll be comin' round the mountain when she comes

Followers:
Here she comes!

For most folks these days, this song brings to mind a sentimental bit of history and speaks of life in 19th century America. Some say that the verse about the red pajamas reminds them of the itchy wool pajamas that were worn by anyone trying to stay warm through the long, cold winters. "Sleeping with Grandma" brings back memories of a time when house sizes were smaller and beds were fewer. In many cases, folk songs are musical histories of life long ago.

She'll Be Comin' Round The Mountain

Traditional

She'll be comin' round the mountain when she comes—Here she comes!
She'll be comin' round the mountain when she comes—Here she comes!
She'll be comin' round the mountain, she'll be comin' round the mountain
She'll be comin' round the mountain when she comes—Here she comes!

She'll be driving six white horses when she comes—Whoa, back!
She'll be driving six white horses when she comes—Whoa, back!
She'll be driving six white horses, she'll be driving six white horses
She'll be driving six white horses when she comes—Whoa, back!

Oh, we'll all go out to meet her when she comes—Hi, Babe!
Oh, we'll all go out to meet her when she comes—Hi, Babe!
Oh, we'll all go out to meet her, we'll all go out to meet her
We'll all go out to meet her when she comes—Hi, Babe!

She'll be wearing red pajamas when she comes—Scratch, scratch!
She'll be wearing red pajamas when she comes—Scratch, scratch!
She'll be wearing red pajamas, she'll be wearing red pajamas
She'll be wearing red pajamas when she comes—Scratch, scratch!

She will have to sleep with Grandma when she comes—Oh, no!
She will have to sleep with Grandma when she comes—Oh, no!
She will have to sleep with Grandma, she will have to sleep with Grandma
She will have to sleep with Grandma when she comes—Oh, no!

We will all have chicken and dumplings when she comes—Yum! Yum!
We will all have chicken and dumplings when she comes—Yum! Yum!
We will all have chicken and dumplings, we will all have chicken and dumplings
We will all have chicken and dumplings when she comes—Yum! Yum!

Here she comes!
Whoa, back!
Hi, Babe!
Scratch, scratch!
Oh, No!
Yum, Yum!

She'll be comin' round the mountain when she comes
She'll be comin' round the mountain when she comes
She'll be comin' round the mountain, she'll be comin' round the mountain
She'll be comin' round the mountain when she comes!